A Note to Parents and Caregivers:

Read-it! Readers are for children who are just starting on the amazing road to reading. These beautiful books support both the acquisition of reading skills and the love of books.

 The PURPLE LEVEL presents basic topics and objects using high frequency words and simple language patterns.

 The RED LEVEL presents familiar topics using common words and repeating sentence patterns.

 The BLUE LEVEL presents new ideas using a larger vocabulary and varied sentence structure.

 The YELLOW LEVEL presents more challenging ideas, a broad vocabulary, and wide variety in sentence structure.

 The GREEN LEVEL presents more complex ideas, an extended vocabulary range, and expanded language structures.

 The ORANGE LEVEL presents a wide range of ideas and concepts using challenging vocabulary and complex language structures.

When sharing a book with your child, read in short stretches, pausing often to talk about the pictures. Have your child turn the pages and point to the pictures and familiar words. And be sure to reread favorite stories or parts of stories.

There is no right or wrong way to share books with children. Find time to read with your child, and pass on the legacy of literacy.

Adria F. Klein, Ph.D.
Professor Emeritus
California State University
San Bernardino, California

Editor: Shelly Lyons
Designer: Tracy Davies
Page Production: Ashlee Schultz
Art Director: Nathan Gassman
Associate Managing Editor: Christianne Jones
The illustrations in this book were created with acrylics and colored pencils.

Picture Window Books
5115 Excelsior Boulevard
Suite 232
Minneapolis, MN 55416
877-845-8392
www.picturewindowbooks.com

Library of Congress Cataloging-in-Publication Data
Shaskan, Trisha Speed, 1973-
Lucy's magic wand / by Trisha Speed Shaskan ; illustrated by
Timberlee Myers.
p. cm. — (Read-it! readers)
ISBN-13: 978-1-4048-4080-5 (library binding)
[1. Magic—Fiction. 2. Fairies—Fiction.] I. Myers, Timberlee, ill.
II. Title.
PZ7.S53242Lu 2008
[E]--dc22
2007032902

Lucy's Magic Wand

by Trisha Speed Shaskan

illustrated by Timberlee Myers

Special thanks to our reading adviser:

Adria F. Klein, Ph.D.
Professor Emeritus, California State University
San Bernardino, California

PICTURE WINDOW BOOKS
Minneapolis, Minnesota

Lucy loved to play with her magic wand.

Her parents always said, "Be careful. Wands are for magic."

Lucy tasted her pumpkin soup. She said, "It needs to be stirred." She held her wand like a spoon.

"Be careful," her mom said. "Wands are for magic."

Lucy stirred the soup with her magic wand.

The soup suddenly turned green. It smelled like rotten eggs.

Lucy said, "I want to be a rock-n-roll fairy." She found a pot to use as a drum. She held her wand like a drumstick.

"Be careful," her dad said. "Wands are for magic."

Lucy hit the pot with her magic wand.

The pot exploded into purple puffs of smoke.

Lucy said, "Classical music might be better."

She took a violin from the closet. She held
her wand like a bow.

"Be careful," her mom said. "Wands are
for magic."

Lucy played the violin with her magic wand.

9

Instead of playing music, the violin screamed in her ear.

Lucy held out her wand and said, "I want to visit the neighbors."

"Be careful," her dad said. "Wands are for magic."

Lucy marched next door and used her magic wand to tap on the neighbors' door.

The door disappeared. The neighbors were not happy with Lucy.

Lucy picked up a baseball. She held her wand like a bat.

"Be careful," her mom said. "Wands are for magic."

Lucy hit the ball with her magic wand.

The ball turned into a bird and flew away.

Lucy found an anthill. She sat down next to it. She held her wand like a shovel.

"Be careful," her dad said. "Wands are for magic."

Lucy poked the dirt with her magic wand.

The ants grew as big as Lucy's feet.

Lucy wanted to play fetch. She called for her dog, Dazzle. She held her wand like a stick.

"Be careful," her mom said. "Wands are for magic."

Lucy threw her magic wand.

Dazzle caught the wand. He turned into a frog and hopped away.

"Oh, no!" Lucy cried.

Her mom picked up the wand. She waved it in the air and said, "Great green grass, great thick bog, please turn Dazzle into a dog!" Then she handed Lucy the wand.

"Thank you," Lucy said.

Lucy took the wand. She spun it around like a baton. Then she tossed it into the air.

"Be careful," her dad said. "Wands are for magic."

When the magic wand dropped from the sky, Lucy caught it.

Boom! Bang! Zip! Lucy shrank to the size of her dog.

"Yikes!" she yelled.

Lucy's dad picked up the wand. He waved it in the air and said, "Great white clouds, great blue skies, please make Lucy just the right size!"

"Thank you," Lucy said.

Lucy's mom said, "You know—"

"Wands are for magic," Lucy said.

Lucy's dad said, "You must—"

"Be careful!" Lucy said.

More *Read-it!* Readers

Bright pictures and fun stories help you practice your reading skills. Look for more books at your level.

Benny and the Birthday Gift
The Best Lunch
The Boy Who Loved Trains
Car Shopping
Clinks the Robot
Firefly Summer
The Flying Fish
Gabe's Grocery List
Loop, Swoop, and Pull!
Patrick's Super Socks
Paulette's Friend

Pony Party
Princess Bella's Birthday Cake
The Princesses' Lucky Day
Rudy Helps Out
The Sand Witch
Say "Cheese"!
The Snow Dance
The Ticket
Tuckerbean at Waggle World
Tuckerbean in the Kitchen

On the Web

FactHound offers a safe, fun way to find Web sites related to topics in this book. All of the sites on FactHound have been researched by our staff.

1. Visit *www.facthound.com*

2. Type in this special code:
   140484080X

3. Click on the FETCH IT button.

Your trusty FactHound will fetch the best sites for you!
A complete list of *Read-it!* Readers is available on our Web site:
www.picturewindowbooks.com

24